An unfamiliar knock shakes
my bedroom door,
I didn't expect anyone today,
my chest begins to roar.

I sneak around the corner
to take a little peek,
a lady short and sweet
is here to speak.

Ms. Duck she is called,
walks over to me.
"I am here to bring you to a new home,
there's no need to flee."

The thought of leaving my home
is not for me,
I'm happy, I'm content,
can't you see?

She says, "this family needs to be
separated until you can all heal"
but the thought of this
makes me want to squeal.

"It's time to go, no more delay,"
my heart is aching as I am led away.

I have never left my home,
I feel so alone.

Ms. Duck says, "let's each take a deep breath
and I'll help you find a way to forgive,
and that's when your family
will start to live."

I leave my Fox family, bed,
and toys with fright,
without a hug or even
a kiss goodnight.

Ms. Duck lovingly says
that I will be okay,
with a family of Bears is
where I will stay.

But I'm a FOX, I'm not a BEAR,
and I just can't help but to despair.

I think about how they
are all brown and I'm all red.
When I think too much
it hurts my head.

I may not look like them,
but I'll still be true,
and show that this Fox can be
part of their crew.

I'll be sure to show them respect
and kindness every day,
and I will make the
most of my stay.

As we approach the Bear's house,
though I'm shaking and scared,
Ms. Duck is there to hold my hand.
Telling me I'm brave and prepared.

I take a deep breath and ring the bell.
Who is coming to the door I cannot tell.

The door starts to open
and smiles fill the air,
I start to see a big
and loving Bear.

A father Bear with glasses so bright,
greets me with a friendly sight.

A mother Bear with a warm embrace,
gives me a hug and squeezes my face.

Their home is cozy and so inviting,
a place of rest is not so frightening.

The Bears show me love and care,
and make me feel like I live here.

Mama and Papa Bear are nice to meet, their son and daughter are just as sweet.

Ms. Duck with a hug, she says goodbye, she'll see me in the morning, no need to cry.

Off to play with my new friends,
this I will do,
I'll be back with a smile,
so I say "toodaloo."

We hop, skip, jump
and be free,
until Mama and Papa Bear say
dinner time is now and we must flee.

There is casserole and salad,
grilled and fried,
there is a lot of variety
I have to try.

They cook up carrots, potatoes,
and some meat,
I have never seen
such a feast.

I look up at the Bears,
and don't know what to say,
I want to eat it all, but my
new friends are more interested in play.

They ask me if I want
any other treat,
I can't refuse... a yummy chocolate chip
cookie is hard to beat.

The Bears tell me that
it's time to rest.
My day has been long,
and that it's for the best.

I say good night to the children
excited for tomorrow,
with my new friends,
there will be no sorrows.

Mama and Papa Bear have come
to tuck me in,
they read me a bedtime story,
it is a win!

Their smile and laughter, fill the air,
a warm feeling inside me, I can tell they care.

I have never slept alone,
but Mama and Papa Bear make
me feel like I am home.

The bedtime story is done,
and they kiss my head goodnight.
My bed is so cozy,
then they flicker off the light.

My eyes grow heavy,
and I begin to drift away,
this home is not so bad,
I may even want to stay.

The End